To We Need Diverse Books and Jim Averbeck — *D. L.*

All my thanks and love go out to my mom, who's a constant support
in my life, as well as my childhood friends Kriti, Cristina, and Bridget,
who taught me even as life changes friendships last forever — *L. S.*

Henry Holt and Company, *Publishers since 1866*
Henry Holt® is a registered trademark of Macmillan Publishing Group, LLC.
120 Broadway, New York, NY 10271 mackids.com

Library of Congress Cataloging-in-Publication Data is available
ISBN 978-1-250-77818-5
Our books may be purchased in bulk for promotional, educational,
or business use. Please contact your local bookseller or the Macmillan
Corporate and Premium Sales Department at (800) 221-7945 ext. 5442
or by email at MacmillanSpecialMarkets@macmillan.com.
First Edition, 2021

Printed In China by RR Donnelley Asia Printing Solutions Ltd.,
Dongguan City, Guangdong Province

The art for this book was drawn with pencil, colored in with ink, scanned,
and then digitally collaged together in Photoshop.

10 9 8 7 6 5 4 3 2 1

FRIENDS
ARE FRIENDS,
FOREVER

By **DANE LIU**

Illustrated by **LYNN SCURFIELD**

GODWINBOOKS

Henry Holt and Company · New York

In our town, the winter howls.
Heavy flakes swarm and glaze the earth.

KISH
SKISH—

Yueyue and I slide, holding on to each other.
She is my neighbor and my best friend.
Together, we teeter and shimmy and giggle to school.

Days before Lunar New Year,
my parents say we're moving—far away.

"Dandan, will you come back?" Yueyue asks.

I kick snow.
"I don't know."

On Lunar New Year's Eve, the grown-ups
bustle, their faces swallowed by steam.
Crunchy vegetables skid around the wok.
Flame-red chilies speckle silky noodles.
Batches of dumplings jiggle in boiling water.

Nainai fishes us our dumplings.
"Eat more tonight." She wipes her eyes
with the corner of her apron.
"So you never forget Nainai's dumplings."

We dip them in black vinegar and soy sauce.
We bite into the egg-and-chive filling.

"Mmmmm!" Yueyue licks her lips.
"The best," I say.

Nainai's stories chime in my ears.
Garlic and ginger tickle my nose.
I close my eyes to remember everything.

When the grown-ups start their card game,
Yueyue pokes me. She and I have our own
New Year's Eve tradition.
We pleat red papers,
zigzag our scissors, and unfold.

We sink our cutouts in water,
stretch strings across the metal plates,
and step carefully into the cold.

"Our best snowflakes yet," Yueyue says.
"And my last." My voice shivers.

HISS
BOOM
CRACK–

She grabs my hand and pulls me
toward the flashing fireworks.

At dawn, our families sleep.
Yueyue and I race.

We knock on our plates—

CLONK!

The circles pop out.
We hang our ornaments high and proud,
and watch them spin
and shimmer in the sunlight.

"I got you something," Yueyue says.
A stack of red paper. A spool of string.
"So you can make cutouts
with a new friend in America."

Yueyue and I hug, not letting go.
She whispers, *"Friends are friends, forever."*

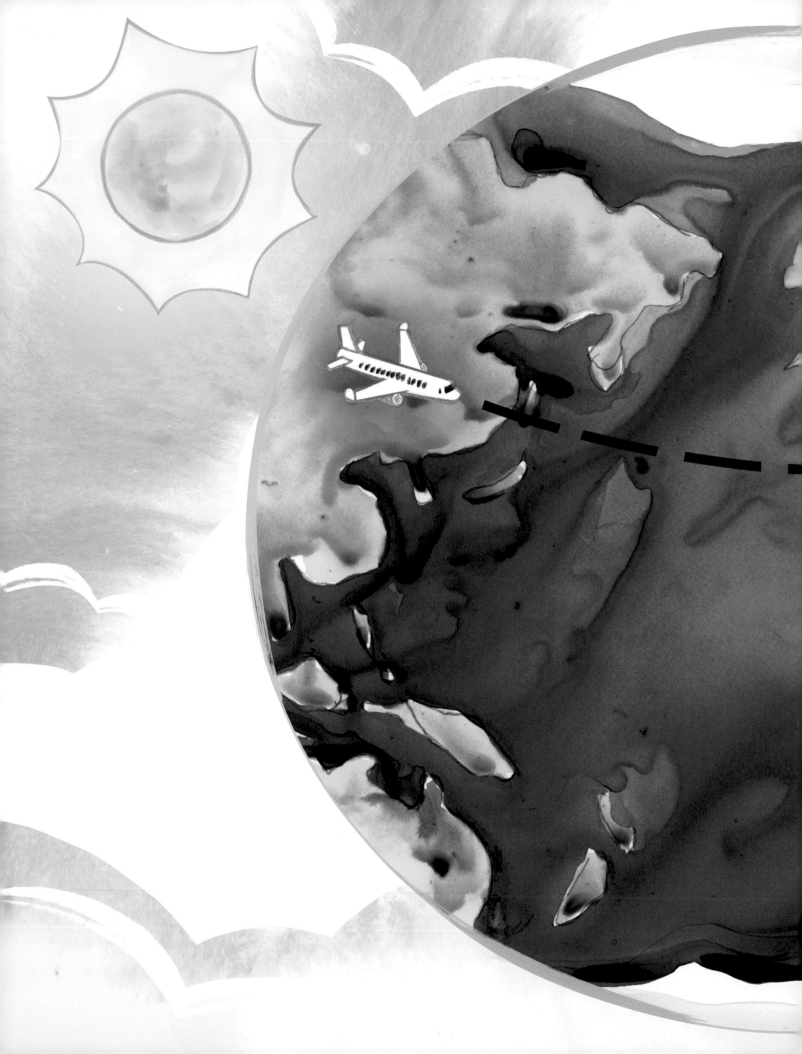

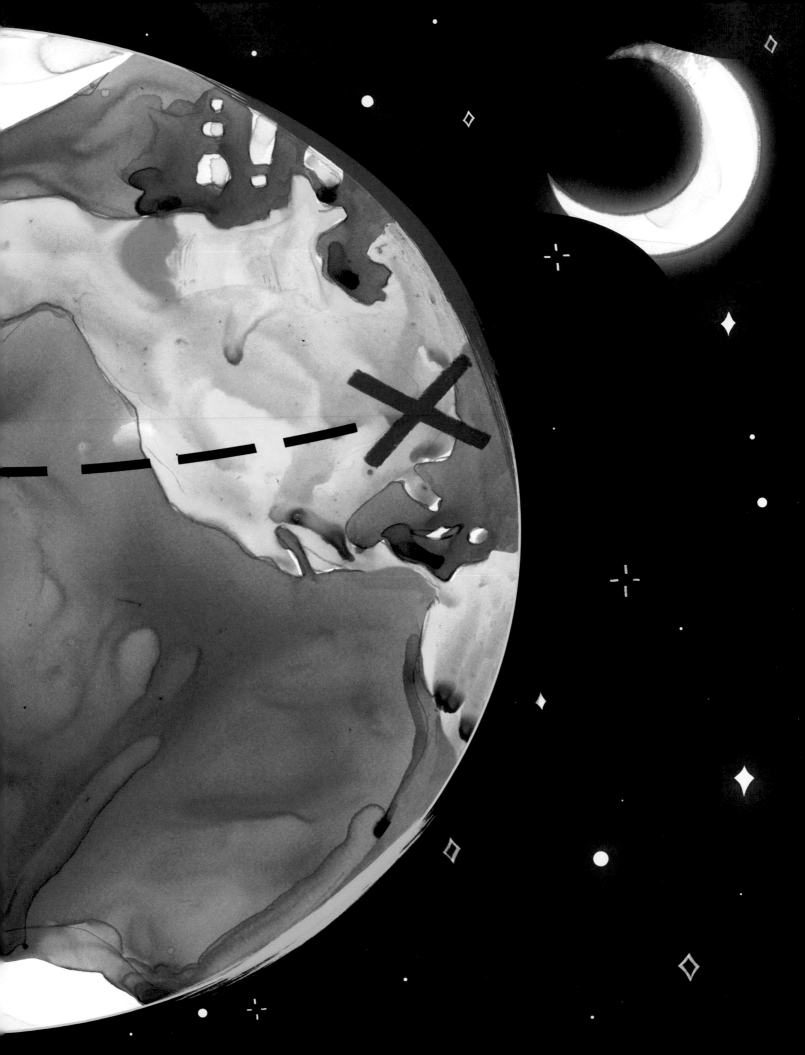

No more breakfasts at Grandma Tai's cart,
dipping fresh crullers in hot,
honeyed soy milk.

Here, I eat alone.

No more threading through traffic,
honking and hollering.

Here, streets are roomy and neat.

No more dreaming to the neighbors'
laughter and checkmates—
our courtyard lullaby.

Here, nights are silent and still.

I watch other kids slide.
I hear them giggle.
But when I come near, the circles close,
and I can't say anything.

I race—
to learn a hundred words a day.
Sometimes I get ten, sometimes only three.

Every night, I fall asleep hugging
a list and my dictionary.

Winter comes.

Leaves fall. No snow.
I tuck Yueyue's gift deep
under my bed.

On my birthday, I wear a satin dress.
My classmates snicker.

"You look awesome." A girl smiles.
She shows me her artwork.
"Red's my favorite color, too."

Christina and I share an easel.

She untangles words
that my dictionary does not.

We build forts and whisper our secrets.

Cheesy Silly Cool

With Christina, my voice blooms.

"Remember this?" She raises her hand.

"High five!" I say.

We clap our palms and giggle.

On Lunar New Year's Eve, my parents bustle
in the kitchen. We peek under my bed.

"What is it?" Christina asks.

I remember Yueyue's wish and slowly take out the bundle.

I show Christina how to pleat,
zigzag, and unfold.

"Beautiful," she says.
"But we can't freeze them," I tell her.
"It's not cold here."
"How 'bout the freezer?" She nudges me.
"Great!"

We dunk our cutouts in cake pans
and slide them in.

That night, I pour black vinegar and soy sauce onto Christina's plate, and rubber band her chopsticks, the way I learned.

We eat steaming dumplings, play cards
with Mama and Baba, and laugh.

At dawn, we dash
to the grumbling machine and knock
on the pans—

CLONK!

We hang our ornaments high and proud,
and watch them glisten and melt.

"I like Lunar New Year." Christina smiles.
"I like being your friend."

"Me too." I stand a little taller.

"Friends are friends, forever."

AUTHOR'S NOTE

In the Chinese tradition,
the grandest holiday is the Lunar New Year, commonly
known as the Chinese New Year or the Spring Festival. The date is determined
by the lunar calendar and occurs in January or February on the Gregorian
calendar. Because China is a vast country with many climates and cultures, people
celebrate the New Year in their distinct regional ways. In the Northeast, where I grew up, families
come together to eat dumplings and play cards. Children make red paper cutouts, freeze
them outside, and hang them as ornaments. In every part of China, it is a
time of celebration and family reunion. The auspicious color
of red is prominently displayed, symbolizing our
wish for good fortune and happiness
in the year ahead.

ABOUT THE AUTHOR

I grew up in Changchun,
a city in Northeastern China. Every morning,
my best friend Yueyue and I giggled our way to school. When my
family and I moved to North Carolina, the transition was hard. I did not speak
English, and the cultural differences were immense. Christina was my first American friend.
We became inseparable. Our friendship taught me that the need to share, respect,
and love is deeply human. It transcends culture, language, background,
and race. Friends like Yueyue and Christina gave me some of my
dearest memories and taught me an enduring truth:
Friends are friends, forever.

ABOUT PAPER CUTTING

Paper cutting has been a beloved folk art in China for nearly 2,000 years. During celebrations such as birthdays, weddings, and the Lunar New Year, people adorn their homes with delicate cuttings. Popular subjects include peony for fortune, peach for long life, fish for abundance, and the zodiac animal of the New Year. There are no limits to the design. The more cuts you make, the more intricate the patterns—a partnership between your hands and your imagination.

TO MAKE A SNOWFLAKE:

1. Begin with a square sheet of paper.

2. Fold it in half to make a rectangle.

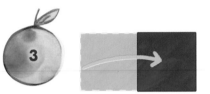

3. Fold it in half to make a square.

4. Fold it in half to make a triangle.

5. Fold it in half one more time to make a skinnier triangle.

6. Snip off the double-pointed side of the triangle. This cut can be straight or curved.

7. Cut into the folded side of the paper however you'd like. The smaller and more numerous the cuts, the more detailed your pattern.

8. When you're done, slowly unfold your snowflake.*

*Like in nature, every snowflake is unique. The smallest change in how you fold or cut the paper will produce a whole new snowflake. How exciting!